First published 2012 by Macmillan Children's Books
a division of Macmillan Publishers Limited
20 New Wharf Road, London N1 9RR
Basingstoke and Oxford. Associated companies throughout the world
www.panmacmillan.com
ISBN: 978-0-230-76368-5
Text and illustrations copyright © Chloë and Mick Inkpen 2012
Moral rights asserted. All rights reserved.
1 3 5 7 9 8 6 4 2
A CIP catalogue record for this book is available from the British Library.
Printed in China

# Hello Oscar!

## Zoe and Beans

### Chloë & Mick Inkpen

MACMILLAN CHILDREN'S BOOKS

Beans had found
something exciting at the
bottom of the garden.

It was small and squeaky
with tufty hair.

A guinea pig!

'Woof!' said Beans.
'Squeak,' said the guinea pig.

And off they went to find a carrot.

$W$hen they came back there was another guinea pig in the garden!

And a **tortoise!**

Zoe had never seen a real tortoise before.

'I wonder if it likes carrot too?' said Zoe.

But Beans had found something even more interesting...

. . . a chameleon!

# Wow!

The chameleon began
to change colour!
Its long, thin tongue
poked in and out.
'Are you hungry?' said Zoe.
'What do chameleons eat?'
she wondered, and she rushed
inside to Google it.

'Live crickets!' said Zoe as she came back outside.
    'Where am I going to find live...'

. . . There was
a **parrot** in the bush!

'This morning I had
just one pet, and now I've got
   two guinea pigs,
a tortoise,
   a chameleon,
a parrot...

   ...and Beans!'

(But where was Beans?)

'Hello Oscar!' said the parrot.
It was a **talking** parrot!

'My name's Zoe actually,'
said Zoe. 'Can you say, "Hello Zoe."'

'Hello Oscar!'
said the parrot.

It flew further into the garden.

'Hello Zoe,' said Zoe.
'Hello Oscar,' said the parrot.

'Hello Zoe,' said Zoe.
'Hello Oscar,' said the parrot.

'Hello Zoe,' said Zoe.
'Hello Oscar,' said the parrot.

This parrot wasn't as clever
as it looked.

Zoe spelt out the letters.

Hello

The parrot looked blank,
then opened its beak and said,

'Hello Oscar'.

Z o e

'My name's not Oscar!

It's Zoe!

Zoe!

Zoe!'

I think I've got your dog.

(It wasn't the parrot talking!)

Woof!
Woof!
Woof!

There was Beans!

And not just Beans.
A rabbit.
A duck.
And a face!
A friendly face.
'Nice dog!'
said the face.

The face disappeared and a moment later a little bottom began wiggling backwards through the hole. Then a stripey jumper...

. . . and lots and lots of curly hair.

'Hello, I'm Oscar!'

'Hello Oscar!' said Zoe.